E
K

King, Larry L.

Because of Lozo
Brown

$11.95

BECAUSE OF LOZO BROWN

By Larry L. King

BECAUSE OF LOZO BROWN

Illustrated by Amy Schwartz

Z4111 9/90
Viking Kestrel

VIKING KESTREL
Published by the Penguin Group
Viking Penguin Inc., 40 West 23rd Street, New York, New York 10010, U.S.A.
Penguin Books Ltd, 27 Wrights Lane, London W8 5TZ England
Penguin Books Australia Ltd, Ringwood, Victoria, Australia
Penguin Books Canada Ltd, 2801 John Street, Markham, Ontario, Canada L3R 1B4
Penguin Books (N.Z.) Ltd, 182–190 Wairau Road, Auckland 10, New Zealand

Penguin Books Ltd, Registered Offices: Harmondsworth, Middlesex, England

First published in 1988 by Viking Penguin Inc.
Published simultaneously in Canada
Text copyright © Texhouse Corporation, 1988
Illustrations copyright © Amy Schwartz, 1988
All rights reserved

Library of Congress Cataloging in Publication Data
King, Larry L., 1933–
Because of Lozo Brown/by Larry L. King; illustrated by Amy Schwartz.
p. cm.
Summary: A little boy is afraid to meet his new neighbor, Lozo Bown, until they begin to play and become friends.
ISBN 0-670-81031-2
[1. Friendship—Fiction.]   I. Schwartz, Amy, ill.   II. Title.
PZ7.K5856Be 1988
[E]—dc 19   88-3952   CIP

Color separations by Imago Ltd., Hong Kong
Printed in Hong Kong by South China Printing Company
Set in Melior
1   2   3   4   5   92   91   90   89   88

For two sweet dumplings:
Lindsay Allison King & Blaine Carlton King
L.L.K.

He moved next door last Thursday
He's new to my hometown.
I'm afraid to go and meet him
That big boy Lozo Brown.

Now I'm afraid to go to school.
I don't *dare* to go downtown.
I may stay indoors forever
. . . Because of Lozo Brown.

Oh, I wish he had not moved next door
Or even to my street!
Or even to this town, or state!
I wish we *never* had to meet!

I'll pull a blanket over my head
And spend the next three years in bed
(Except to sneak downstairs for jelly-bread)
. . . Because of Lozo Brown.

He's bigger than a tree house.
He's taller than a post.
The ground shakes where he walks on it
That's what scares me most.

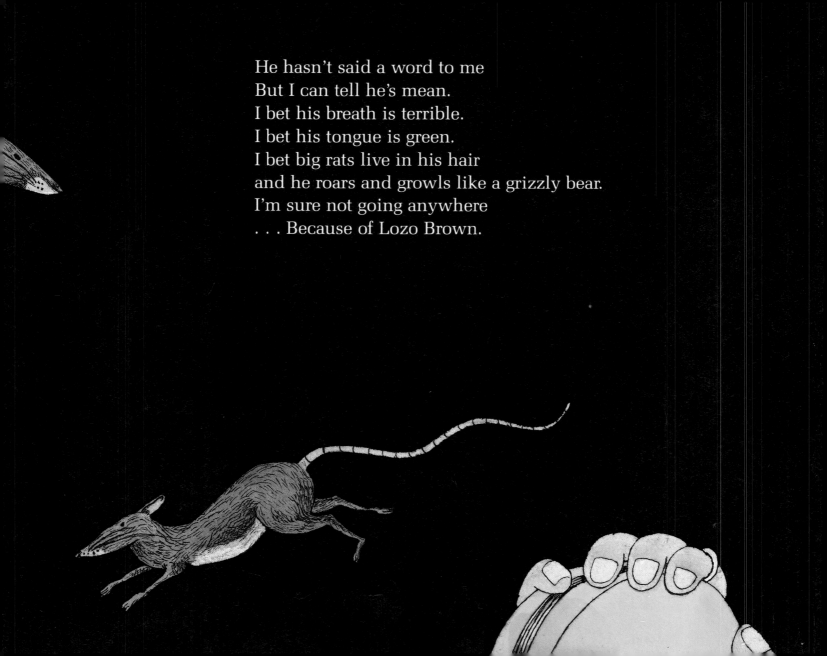

He hasn't said a word to me
But I can tell he's mean.
I bet his breath is terrible.
I bet his tongue is green.
I bet big rats live in his hair
and he roars and growls like a grizzly bear.
I'm sure not going anywhere
. . . Because of Lozo Brown.

I'll bet you anything he likes to fight.
He'll probably try to steal my kite.
I worry about such things all night
. . . Because of Lozo Brown.

My mother says his mom's real nice.
My dad and his talked once or twice.
But I'd rather eat a bowl of mice
than meet that Lozo Brown.

Oh no! He's looking in my window!
He's just yelled "Come out and play!"
I'll pretend I didn't see him.
Maybe then he'll go away.

Mom is coming up the stairs!
She's calling my full name!
Telling me to dress and go outdoors
To play some stupid game.

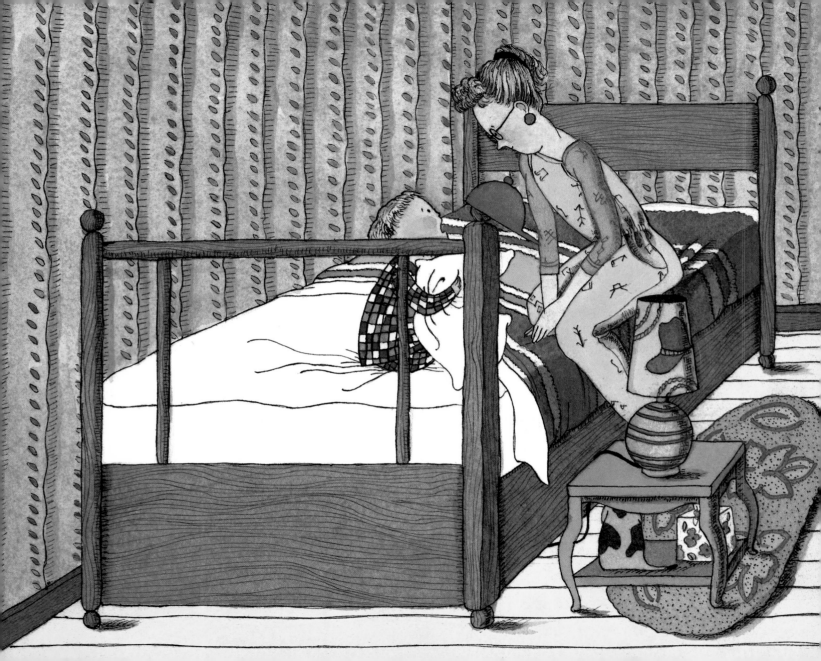

I *told* Mom he's a pirate
And a ghost who changes shapes
And a giant who gobbles other boys
Like they were jelly-cakes!
She laughed and called me "silly sweets"
and ruffled up my hair.
But I bet that she'll be sorry
When I vanish in thin air.

I want *you* to listen carefully, now,
To what I have to say:
If I'm not back here mighty quick
You do *this* for me, OK?

Go tell some nice policeman
To search the whole wide town.
And that I'm among the missing
. . . Because of Lozo Brown.

Good-bye, I must go meet him
Though I know he'll break my nose
And take my good-luck penny
And stomp on my poor toes.

Wait! Don't call that policeman!

I've had a change of heart!
I've been playing with my neighbor
And he's quite a *friendly* sort!

He's let me pet his kitten
And feed his tropical fish.
He's shared his toys and everything
A brand-new friend could wish!

When school lets out tomorrow
His mom's taking us downtown

We'll eat ice cream and have big fun

. . . Because of Lozo Brown.